DC LEAGUE OF SUPER-PETS

THE OFFICIAL
ACTIVITY BOOK

Random House 🏠 New York

All rights reserved. Published in the United States by Random House Children's Books, a division of Penguin Random House LLC, 1745 Broadway, New York, NY 10019, and in Canada by Penguin Random House Canada Limited, Toronto. Random House and the colophon are registered trademarks of Penguin Random House LLC.
ISBN 978-0-593-43196-2 (trade)
rhcbooks.com
Printed in the United States of America
10 9 8 7 6 5 4 3 2 1

KRYPTO

THE SUPER-DOG IN TRAINING

Krypto came to Earth as a puppy, in a rocket ship with a baby from the planet Krypton. Unscramble the words to learn the superpowers of this Super-Dog in training!

A T E H   S N I O V I

P R E S U

R A I G H E N

L I F T G H

Z E F E E R

T H A B E R

R O S A L   A W P   C H U N P

Krypto's best friend is Superman,
a Super Hero from another planet!
What is Superman's secret identity?
To reveal the answer, follow the lines and
write each letter in the correct box.

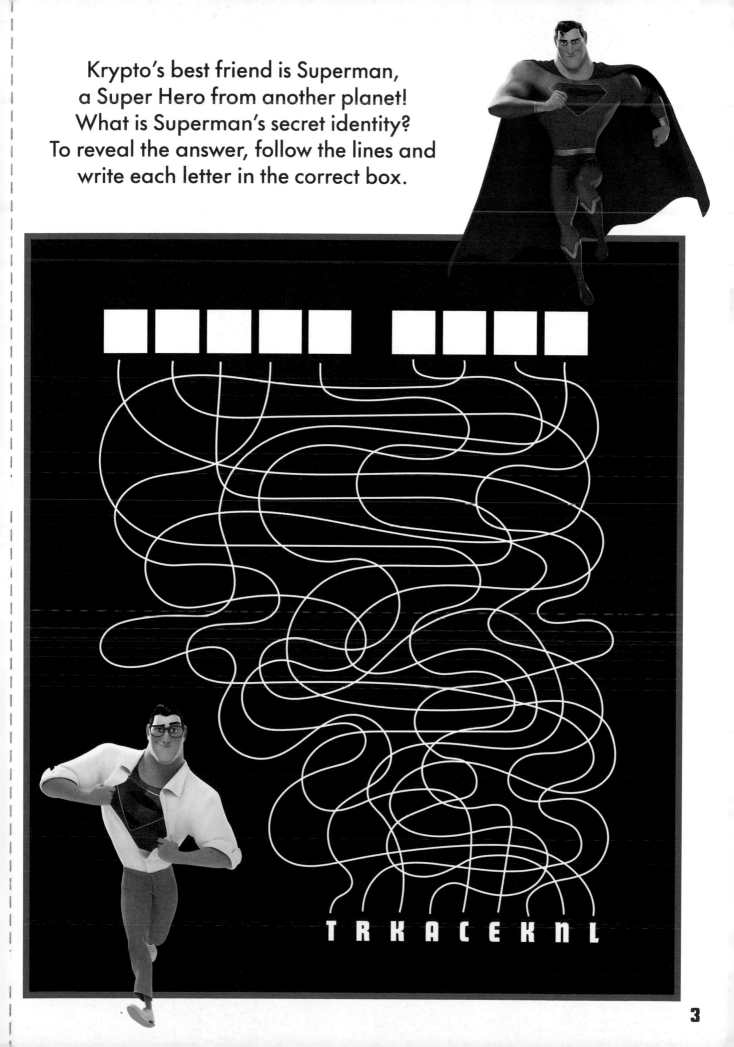

TRKACEKNL

Superman and Krypto live in the city of Metropolis.
How many words can you make using the letters in

METROPOLIS?

_____   _____   _____

_____   _____   _____

_____   _____   _____

_____   _____   _____

_____   _____   _____

Where does Superman go to find a new friend for Krypto?
To answer the question, solve the maze and write the letters along the correct path in order in the boxes.

START

FINISH

ACE is a loner dog who Krypto befriends—and so does Batman!

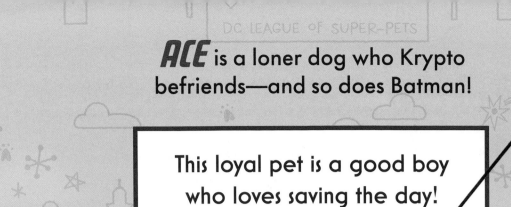

This loyal pet is a good boy who loves saving the day!

What is Ace's superpower?
Use the key to decode the answer!
Write the letters on the blanks.

KEY

A	B	C	D	E	F	G	H	I	J	K	L	M

N	O	P	Q	R	S	T	U	V	W	X	Y	Z

PB is a growing pig—that's her superpower! She can change her size!

This wonder pig loves to snuggle. And her size-changing ability means she can adjust to any size snuggle Wonder Woman wants!

Use the key to color this picture of PB.

KEY
1 = brown   3 = pink   5 = red
2 = gold   4 = blue   6 = tan

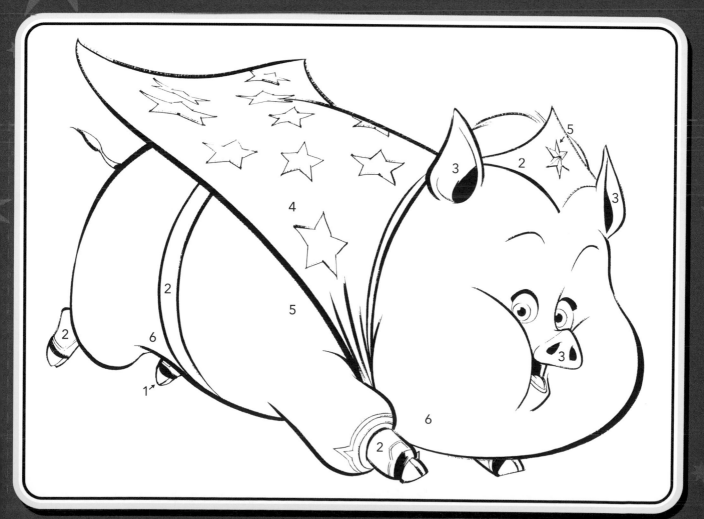

Merton is the Fastest Turtle Alive!
She's super-fast—and not just for a turtle!

MERTON

Merton loves to eat lettuce and make friends. When she isn't speeding to save the world, she gives terrific high fives!

Merton the turtle has a question for you!
To decode it, change each letter below to
the one that comes before it in the alphabet.
Write the letters in the boxes.

IPX GBTU DBO ZPV HP?

Everything changes in a flash of lightning—
and lightning is **Chip's** superpower!

Have you ever
wanted to hug a squirrel?
If so, Chip is the pet for you!
This delightful companion just
needs to feel safe and loved.

Look at the first picture carefully.
Then circle 5 things that are different in the second picture.

Lulu is a hairless guinea pig from Lex Luthor's lab. What does she need in order to become what she was always meant to be? To find out, start at the arrow, and, going clockwise around the circle, write every other letter in order in the boxes.

LULU

Lex Luthor is a bad guy who clashes with Superman and Krypto. This villain wants the same thing as Lulu— but *she* knows something Lex doesn't.
Use the key to find out what it is!

LIZMTV PIBKGLMRGV LMOB DLIPH LM ZMRNZOH!

O R A N G E   K R Y P T O N I T E

O N L Y   W O R K S   O N

A N I M A L S !

A	B	C	D	E	F	G	H	I	J	K	L	M	N	O	P	Q	R	S	T	U	V	W	X	Y	Z
Z	Y	X	W	V	U	T	S	R	Q	P	O	N	M	L	K	J	I	H	G	F	E	D	C	B	A

Superman is in the Justice League
with other Super Heroes, like
Aquaman.

This Super Hero can
talk to sea creatures!

Connect the dots to meet a friend Aquaman made on
one of his ocean adventures.

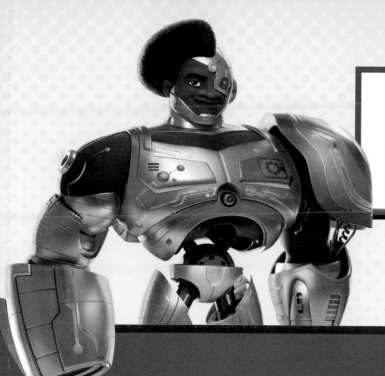

CYBORG is part man, part machine, and all Super Hero!

Use the grid to learn how to draw this Super Hero.

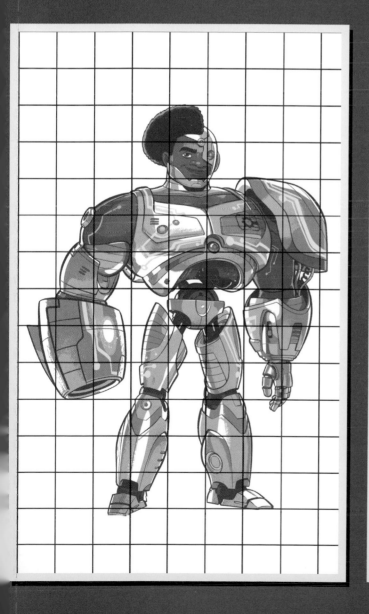

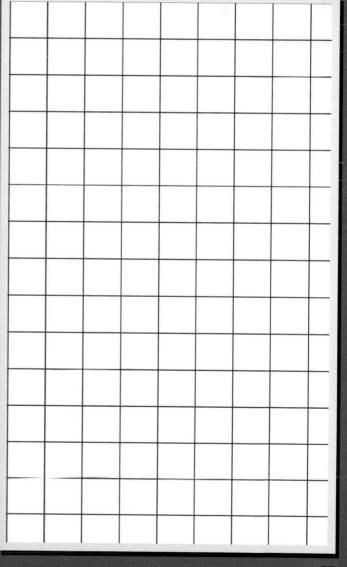

Wonder Woman

is the Justice League's Amazon Warrior!
Solve the maze to help her get
to her Invisible Jet.

START

What do you think the Invisible
Jet looks like? Draw it here!

FINISH

Green Lantern

is an intergalactic
Super Hero!

Where does Green Lantern's
superpower come from?
Use the key to find out!
Write the letters on the blanks.

KEY

A	B	C	D	E	F	G	H	I	J	K	L	M	N	O	P	Q	R	S	T	U	V	W	X	Y	Z

The Flash is faster than the speed of light!

How fast can The Flash get to the Super-Pets? Solve the maze by following the paw prints as fast as you can!

START

FINISH

DC LEAGUE OF SUPER-PETS

It's **Batman**, the Dark Knight!

How do Batman and Ace get around Metropolis?
To find out, connect the dots!

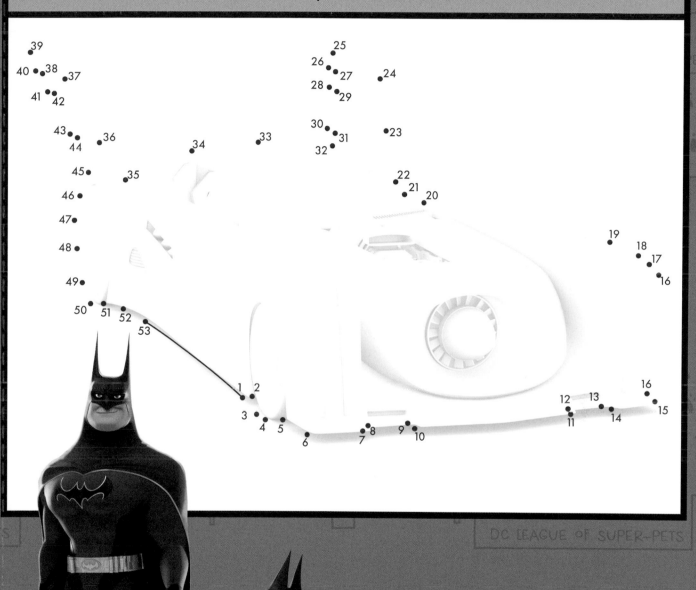

Can you match each pet and person pair
to their correct names?

The Flash  PB

Wonder
Woman  Lulu

Green
Lantern  Ace

Lex Luthor  Merton

Batman  Chip

Superman  Krypto

Draw your own Super-Pet!

Would it be a dog, a cat, a guinea pig, a fish, or something else? What's their superpower? What would their Super Hero name be? Go wild!

METROPOLIS DOTS

With a friend, take turns connecting two dots with a straight line. If the line you draw completes a box, put your initials in it and take another turn. Count one point for squares containing your initials. Boxes containing Super Hero symbols are worth two points. When all the dots have been connected, the player with more points wins!

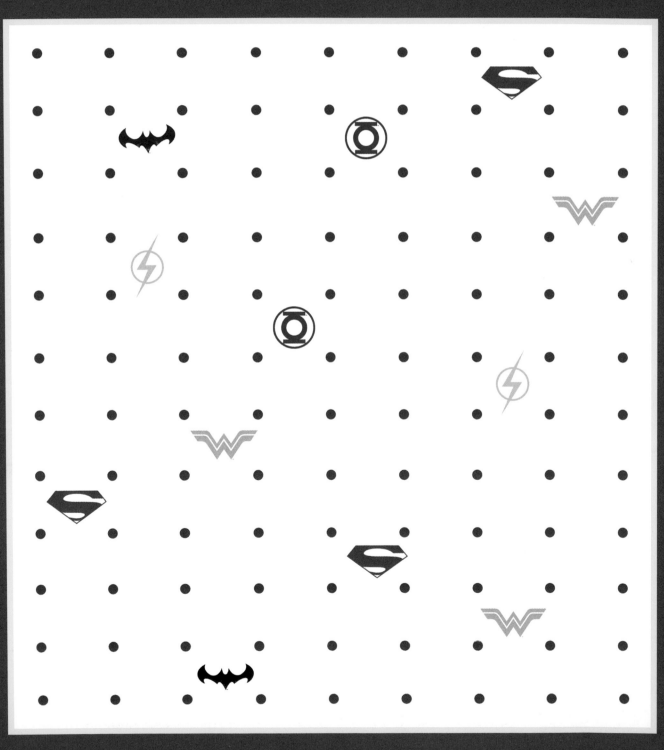

With help from a grown-up, cut out these bookmarks along the dotted lines. Personalize them with your name and stickers!

KRYPTO

MERTON

PB

ACE

CHIP

THIS BOOK BELONGS TO

_____

THIS BOOK BELONGS TO

_____

THIS BOOK BELONGS TO

_____

THIS BOOK BELONGS TO

_____

THIS BOOK BELONGS TO

_____

Study this map of Metropolis for 20 seconds.
Then turn the page and see if you can answer the questions.

Answer the questions to see how much you
remember about the map on the previous page!

What building is closest to Lex Park?

_____

What is the animal shelter called?

_____

Where is the Daily Planet Building? (Hint: It's where Lulu is!)

_____

Where is the Batmobile parked? (Hint: It's close to Ace!)

_____

Which two Super-Pets are closest to each other on the map?

_____

RULE THE WORLD

CHIP

KRYPTO
THE SUPER DOG

POW!

MERTON

Lulu wants to free Lex Luthor! To find out where he is, solve the maze and write the letters along the correct path in order in the boxes.

START

FINISH

25

What are the Super-Pets saying?
Draw and use your stickers to make your own comic panel scenes!

Complete this
DC LEAGUE OF SUPER-PETS

poster with your stickers. Then have a grown-up
help you cut out and hang up this poster
and the poster on the next page!

SUPER POWERED PACK

DC LEAGUE OF SUPER-PETS

The *DC League of Super-Pets*
is off to the rescue. Solve the maze to
help them save the day!

START

FINISH

RODENT ROUNDUP

Lulu's legion of superpowered guinea pigs is wreaking havoc on Metropolis! Can you catch them and save the day? With a friend, take turns connecting two dots with a straight line. If the line you draw completes a box, put your initials in it and take another turn. Count one point for squares containing your initials. When all the dots have been connected, the player with more points wins! Boxes containing paw prints are worth two points!

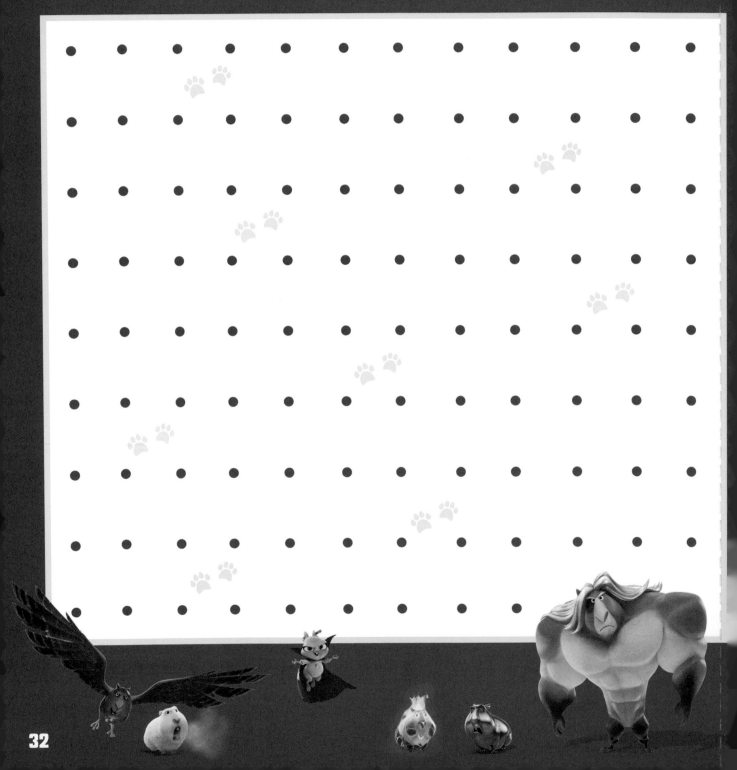

Draw the other half of each Super-Pet's symbol!

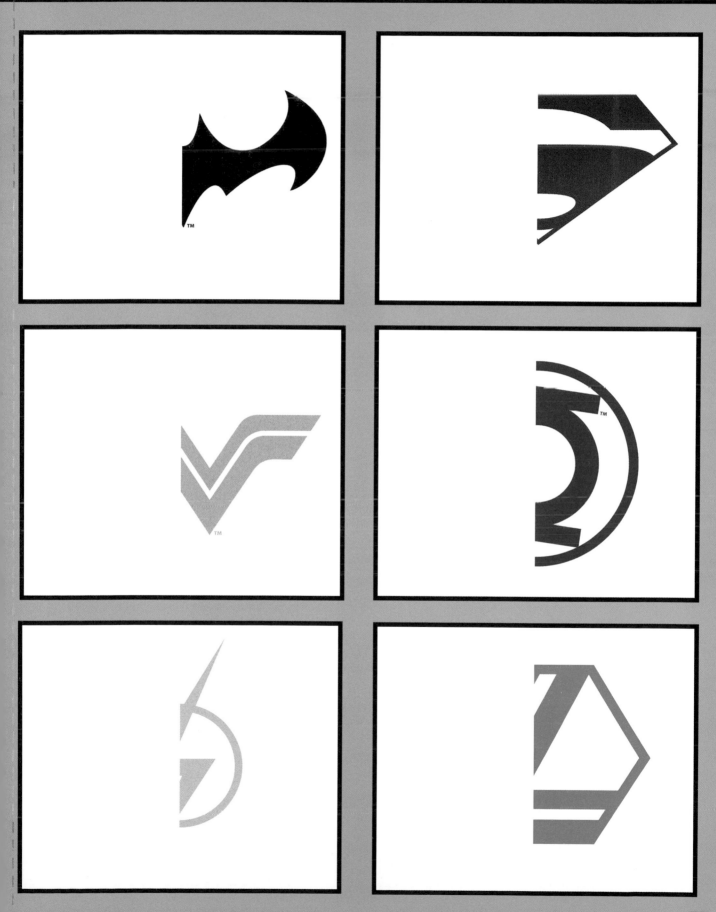

Who is faster?

Using the mazes on this page and the next, start at the same time and race against a friend to see who can reach the Hall of Justice first—The Flash or Merton!

START

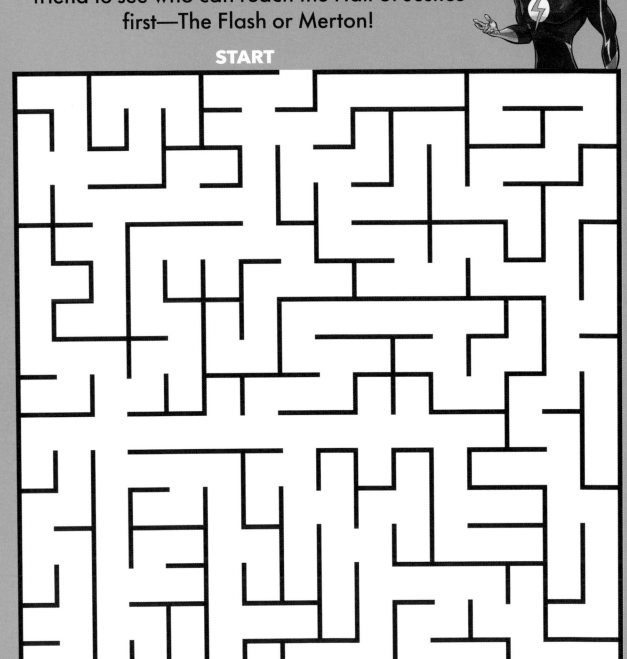

FINISH

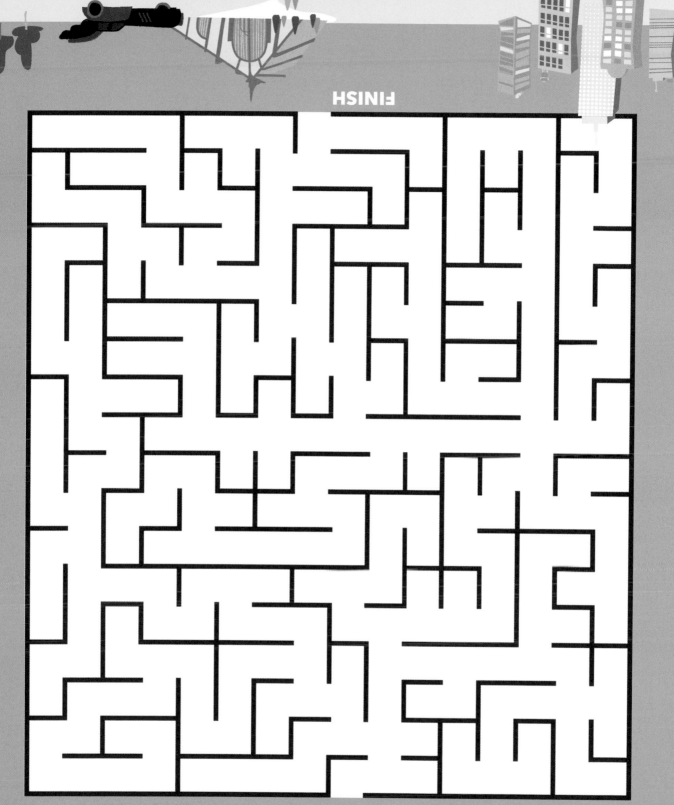

START

Who is faster?

Using the mazes on this page and the next, start at the same time and race against a friend to see who can reach the Hall of Justice first—The Flash or Merton!

Who draws faster?

Use the grid to learn how to draw Krypto! Have a friend draw on the opposite page at the same time and race to see who can finish drawing the Super-Dog first!

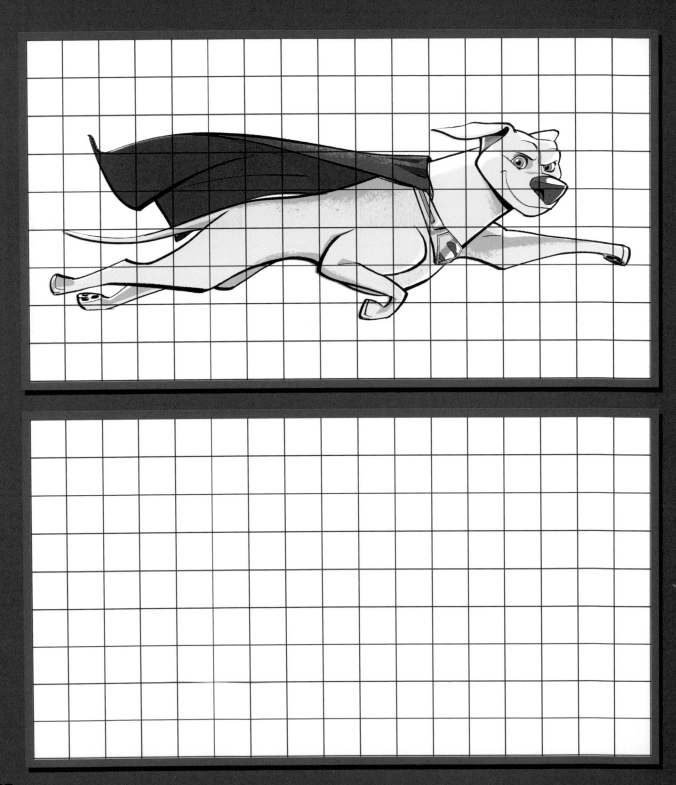

Who draws faster?

Use the grid to learn how to draw Krypto! Have a friend draw on the opposite page at the same time and race to see who can finish drawing the Super-Dog first!

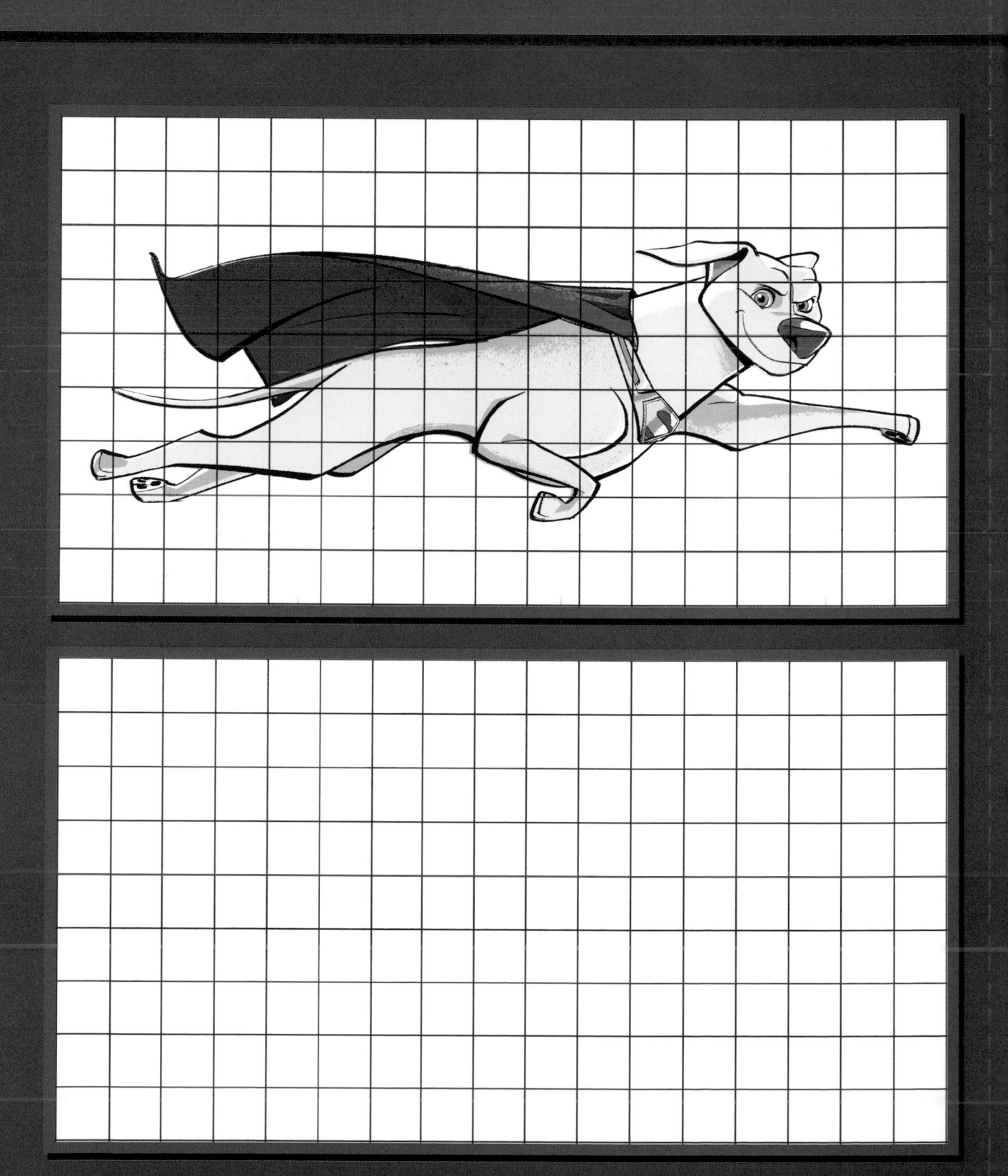

On the next few pages, you'll find pieces of a Super Hero–sized

DC League of Super-Pets poster!

- Carefully remove the next four pages and trim the edges.
- Lay them facedown in the correct order.
- Tape the pages together and hang the poster on your wall!

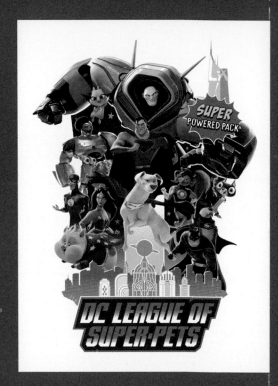

DC
LEAGUE OF
SUPER-PETS

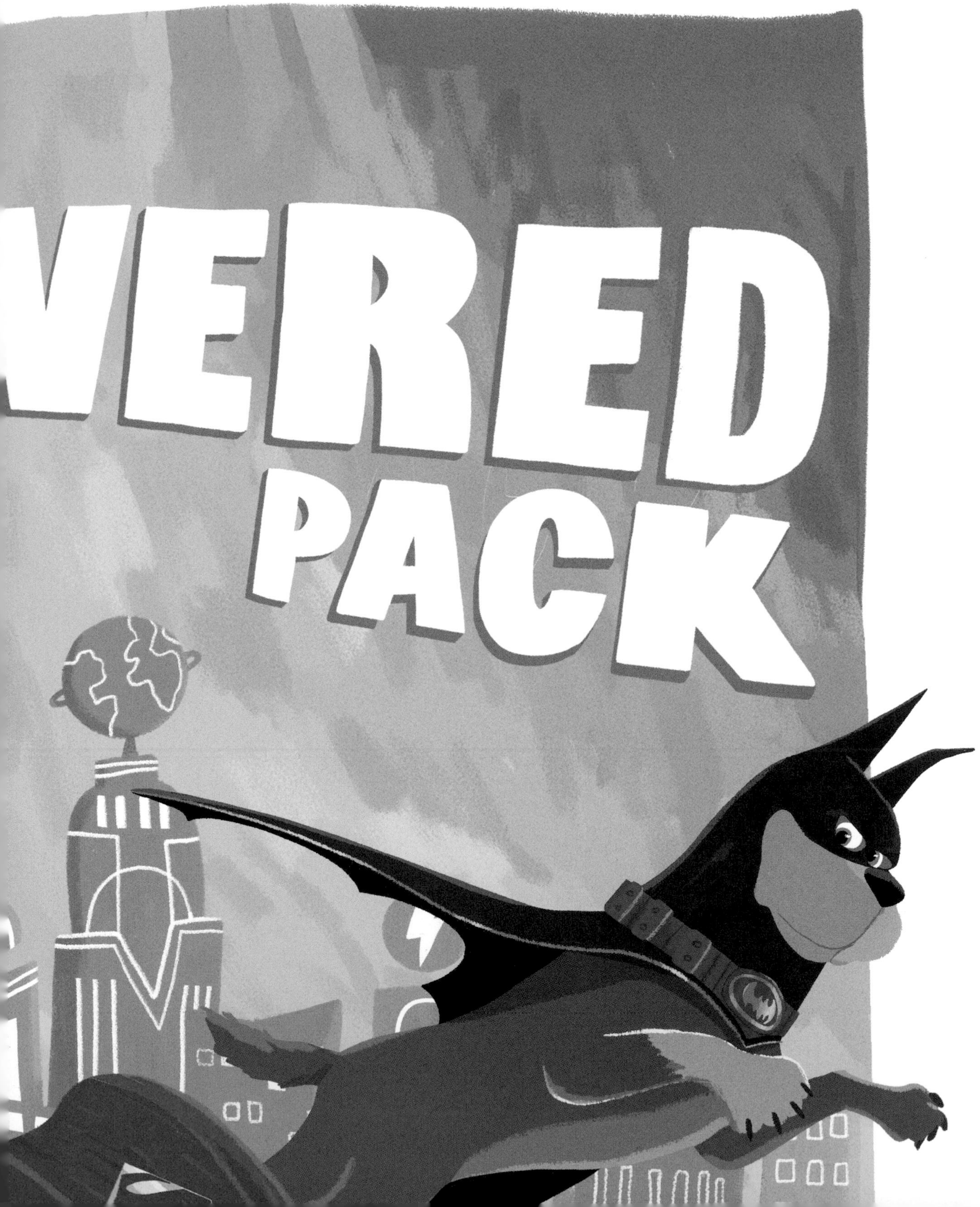
VERED
PACK

OF SUPER-PETS

DC LEAGUE O

ANSWERS

Page 2

heat vision
super-hearing
flight
freeze breath
Solar Paw Punch

Page 3

Clark Kent

Page 4

Possible answers: Let, lime, list, lose, lot, met, mole, moo, mop, more, oil, pet, pile, post, poster, rise, role, room, slip, store, time, tool

Page 5

animal shelter

Page 6

invulnerability

Page 8

"How fast can you go?"

Page 9

• Chip is missing
• a tower is now blue
• another tower is missing its details
• PJ is missing motion lines
• a cloud is now yellow

Page 10

Orange Kryptonite

Page 11

Orange Kryptonite only works on animals!

Page 14

Page 15

her power ring

Page 16

ANSWERS

Page 18

Page 24

1. Lex Tower
2. Tailhuggers
3. Daily Square
4. Hall of Justice
5. Krypto and Lulu

Page 25

Page 31

Pages 34–35